Reebee dedoo dada

Text & Art Copyright © 2022 by Fiely Matias

Published by
Redhawk Publications
The Catawba Valley Community College Press
2550 US Hwy 70 SE
Hickory NC 28602

ISBN: 978-1-952485-85-5

Library of Congress Number: 2022943189

Printed in the United States of America

redhawkpublications.com

For Dennis

In a box on a street
Where two alleys meet
Lived a cat who just loved to sing

And each night around nine
Her friends formed a line
To hear jazzy Zazzie sing swing

The crowds cheered for the cat
Who'd croon and who'd scat
Oh, that sound; a glorious thing!

"Reebee, dedoo, dada

Reebee, dedoo, dadee

Reebee, dedoo, dada

Da, dedoo, dadee"

And in no time at all
Fans flocked to her call
As she warbled under the moon

'Til one night when a rat
A bully, at that
Made a plan to change Zazzie's tune

You see Rex couldn't trill
Like Zazzie with skill
He just couldn't find the right key

So he worked up a scheme
To crush Zazzie's dream:
"No one sings, nobody but me!"

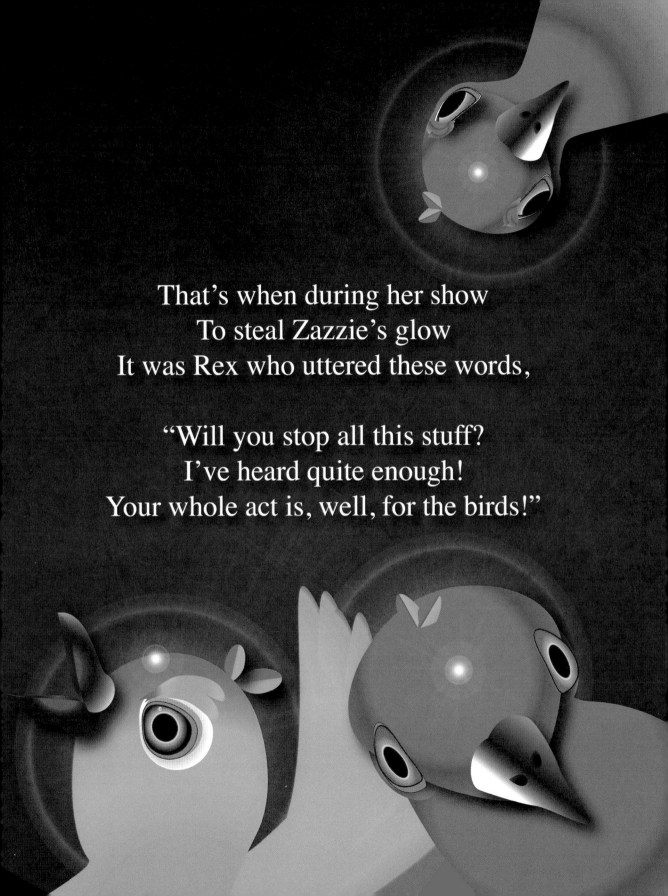

That's when during her show
To steal Zazzie's glow
It was Rex who uttered these words,

"Will you stop all this stuff?
I've heard quite enough!
Your whole act is, well, for the birds!"

That's when everything stopped
And Zazzie's face dropped
She went silent, sad through and through

There was music, then none
Show over, gig done
She just didn't know what to do

Rex had spoiled the event
The crowd up and went
Leaving Zazzie glum and astray

No more Reebee dedoo
The mood had turned blue
As did Zazzie's coat, by the way

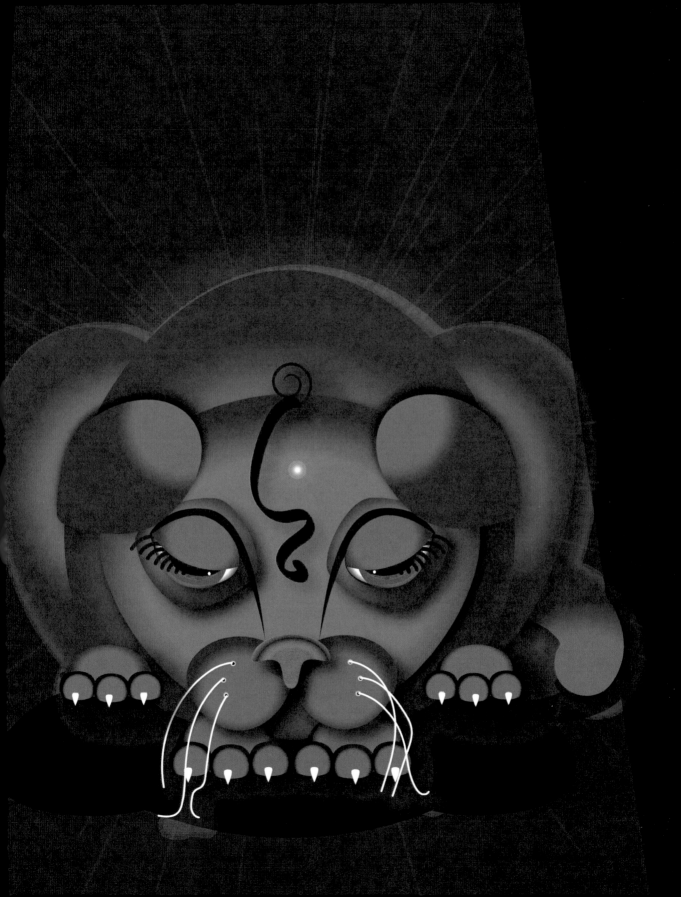

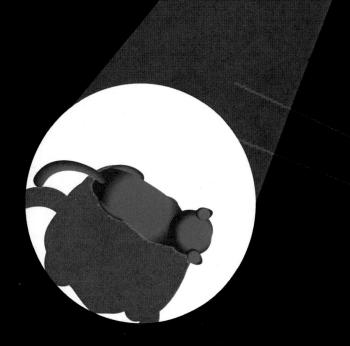

What was em'rald and green
As bright as a bean
Turned a hue, so blue it was bleak

Soon Ms. Zazzie kicked rocks
Slinked home to her box
Where, curled up, she slept for a week

Until Tuesday 'round four
On Zazzie's front door
Came a knocking; one thump, then two

She awoke sleepy-eyed
Peeked out and she spied
Twin gophers in loafers - it's true!

"I'm Delilah! I'm Hope!
Don't cry, please don't mope,
We've a stage we own in the park.

And we pray that you might
Perform there tonight -
Do a show, you know, after dark!"

Though she did love to sing
She still felt the sting
From the night ol' Rex crashed her act

All those words that rat said
Still rang in her head
She was scared she'd fail, that's a fact

"Though my first love's the stage,
  I've since turned the page
    for I'm scared and so filled with doubt.

    I can't purr, I can't croon,
      It's all way too soon
        But I'm grateful you've heard me out."

Now know this, my dear friends
It's key that one lends
A kind ear when someone is down

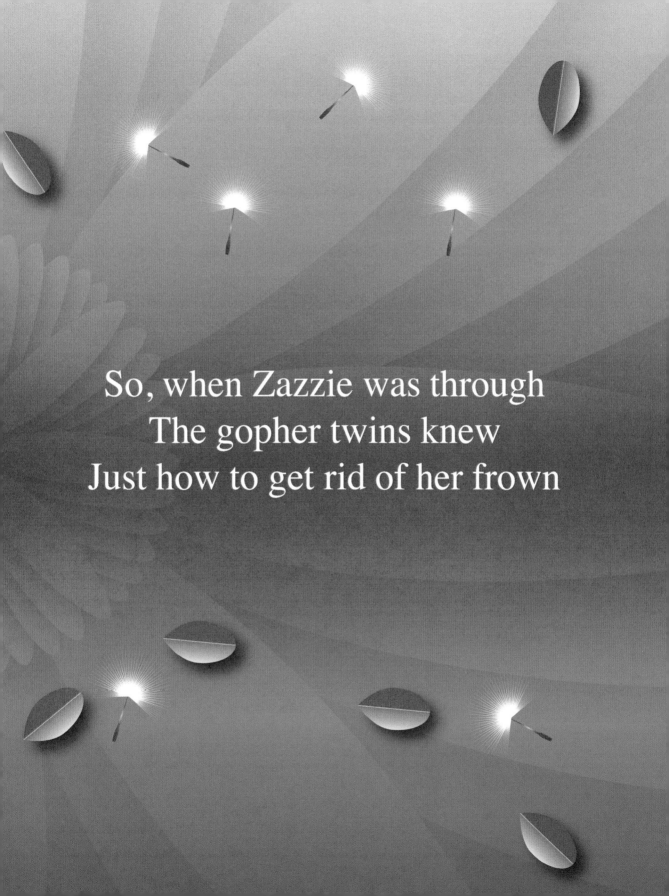

So, when Zazzie was through
The gopher twins knew
Just how to get rid of her frown

"You are seen, you are heard.
Each phrase, every word.
It's healthy to share how you feel."

"Yes, to voice what's inside
With truth as your guide
Is a sure-fire way one can heal."

Hearing this sparked a smile
She beamed for awhile
Say ten minutes, maybe fifteen

Then, in front of their eyes
To Zazzie's surprise
She had changed from blue back to -

GREEN!

"I feel better! I do!
All thanks to you two!"
Said the cat who once again glowed.

And that night in the park
Sometime after dark
With a line clear out to the road -

There was music once more
Sold out, like before
So the gophers lengthened the run

One show became many
First ten, then twenty
All was great until twenty-one

See, that twenty-first night
Gave Zazzie a fright
'Cause Rex had returned with one aim

With a scowl on his face
He planned to disgrace
Jazzy Zazzie's show and good name

But ol' Rex changed his tune
When he heard her croon
Zazzie's singing made his heart melt

Yes, her act was so good
Now Rex understood
And told Zazzie just how he felt:

"Truth is I cannot sing.
It's just not my thing
And I guess I blamed that on you.

In wanting to be seen
I failed, I got mean,
Not a fair thing for me to do.

I'm so sorry, my dear.
I hope you can hear
All the cheers, hurrahs, and applause.

Please forget what I said
And sing out instead!"
Urged Rex as he held Zazzie's paws.

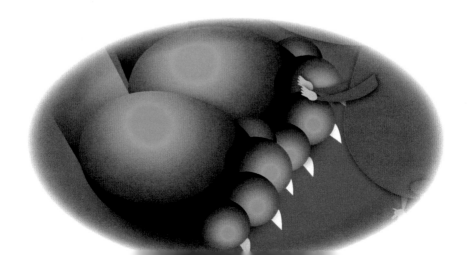

A few moments went by
Before she'd reply
She thought … then was ready to share:

"To forgive is divine.
You sure crossed the line
But I'm touched to know that you care.

So, can't we start anew?
In fact, maybe you
Would consider joining my band.

On the drums or the flute:
That horn needs a toot!
You could sing - hey! That would be grand!"

The rat's eyes welled with tears
The crowd roared with cheers
As Zazzie and Rex shared a hug

They became quite the rave
As this moment gave
Everybody's heart a good tug

Their new show was a smash
And Rex made a splash
It turns out he knew how to dance

He could twirl, he could dip
He'd cartwheel and flip
And the seats sold out in advance

And the two would duet
As he'd pirouette
While everyone sang happily

"Reebee, dedoo, dada...

Reebee, dedoo, dadee...

Reebee, dedoo, dada...

Da, dedoo, dadee!"

And Zazzie
was happy.

kind

respectful

yourself

Let's Talk About It

(A few questions to ask kids to talk about bullying)

1. What is bullying?

2. Have you ever seen anyone being bullied?

3. Have you ever felt you have been bullied?

4. What can you do if you are being bullied?

5. What can you do if you see someone being bullied?

6. Who was being bullied in the book?

7. Who was the bully in the book?

8. Who helped Zazzie in the book?

9. Zazzie loved to sing. What kind of things do you like to do?

10. How would the world be better if no one bullied anyone else?

Stop Bullying Dot Gov   Do Something   Cyber Bullying   Stomp out bullying

About the author

Fiely Matias is a freelance artist who loves theatre, drawing, yoga, photography and dancing. He is awkward, uncomfortable and has a weird sense of humor. He loves the color green, loves to cook and loves to laugh.

Made in the USA
Columbia, SC
24 September 2022

67491251R00044